The Descendants Book 1: The Spear of Destiny

MW01128912

By Daniel Bell

This book is a work of fiction. The views expressed herein are the sole responsibility of the author. Likewise, certain characters, places, and events are the product of the author's imagination, and any resemblance to actual persons, living or dead, or actual events or locales, is entirely coincidental.

Dedication

To all my friends and family who encouraged me to pursue my writing passion. Thank you for all your support; it is much appreciated.

Prologue

A Roman centurion walked up to Jesus Christ as he was hanging on the cross and thrusted his spear against his skin.The moment the blood of Jesus Christ dripped on the spear it became infused with some of his divine power and energy. The Roman centurion, Longinus, did not realize the spear would become an immeasurable weapon with immense power that would later be called "The Spear of Destiny." For generations people have searched for the Spear in order to use its power to accomplish their own goals by any means necessary. At one point, during the generations that followed, the Knights Templar, an organization composed of a group of Christian warriors for God, found the Spear of Destiny located in Jerusalem during the Crusades. They were able to gain wealth and significant influence before they were falsely accused of worshiping Satan and burned to the stake for crimes they didn't commit. As a result, the legendary Spear of Destiny was once again lost to the world. But it suddenly reappeared in the year 1930 when a young Adolf Hitler discovered it in Austria, Hungary. He would then go on to attempt to use the Spear's power and influence to rule Europe and impose his Third Reich. But the spear found him unworthy of its immense power and as a result the spear was lost to him. As World War II continued to wage on, the Allied Forces invaded Germany and discovered the Spear in one of Hitler's hideouts. Hitler knew the war was over because of the spear rejecting him, so he committed suicide. The Allied Forces realized the power of the Spear of Destiny was too great to be controlled by one person or by a group of people, so they split the Spear into three pieces and scattered them throughout different parts of the globe. They hoped the Spear would never again be united—whoever controls the Spear of Destiny controls the world!

Chapter 1: Danny Wallace

Danny Wallace was getting dressed for school. He combed and brushed his hair quickly. He then put hair grease in his hair to make his hair look good. He could see his African skin sweating and his facial hair underneath his chin. So he grabbed his razor and quickly shaved his face getting most if not all the hair gone. He always hated how his facial hair itched his skin, so he felt a sense of relief when he cut off his facial hair. But that didn't matter because today was the day he had been waiting for. He could feel the excitement coming from his face because he was starting his first day of his senior year of high school. After graduation, he would be getting ready to go to college. "I'm going to make the best of my senior year," he thought. He never felt this happy before. The feeling of being so close to being an adult had created a sense of exhilaration in him. He finished getting dressed, grabbed his backpack, and headed towards the door when all of a sudden; he noticed a golden amulet sitting on his bed with a note on it. He picked up the note. Judging by the handwriting, he knew that it was from his mom. It stated, "Hey Danny, your grandfather wanted to give you this as a gift for you becoming a senior. This artifact has been in our family for centuries and passed down for generations and now he wants you to have it. Please take care of it. Love Mom."

Danny grabbed the amulet and took a closer look at it; there was a strange inscription that had Hebrew symbols and markings. He couldn't read it for a second, but then suddenly, it was as if his brain put it all together—like it was natural, and the inscription read "David of Israel."

Danny didn't know why, but he felt a sense of calmness as he was able to read the inscription of the amulet. It was as if he was naturally born to wear it. Whenever he read his Bible and began to study it, he would always go to the book of Kings for David's story. It was as if he could relate to him in some type of way. He placed the amulet around his neck and it immediately felt natural to him, as if it was a part of him now.

He then went back to the task at hand, got the rest of his things, put them in his backpack, and left the house for school. As he was walking to the bus stop, he could hear someone walking behind him. But not in just any kind of way, the kind that feels really creepy, as if he was trying to sneak up on him. Danny saw out the corner of his eye that the mysterious figure had on a black hoody, blue jeans, and a pair of black and gold Jordan shoes. Danny kept on walking at a steady pace, but kept an eye on the hooded figure.

Suddenly the figure started to run towards him with an object—he couldn't see clearly what it was. With haste, the figure leaped and tried touch him in the back of his head, but Danny used his quick reflexes to his advantage.

He moved slightly to his left, dodged the figure's attack, and put out his right leg to trip the figure. The boy then fell to the ground with a thud and let out a light scream. Then he said, "Danny, you didn't have to trip me like that."

The boy got up and pulled off his hood. He was African American with dreadlocks and a dog tag cross on his neck. He was clearly well built from head to toe. Danny recognized him immediately, it was his friend, Samuel Corbin, or Sam for short.

Danny sighed with a sense of relief and said, "Hey Sam, you're going to have to do better next time if you want to spook me."

"Okay, I will. Anyway, are you excited for senior year man?"

"Yeah, I can't wait."

"Yeah, we have to end it off with a bang."

"You know it."

Danny and Sam watched as other students appeared. When they appeared, Danny and Sam would go and talk to them. Both of them were very outgoing people and they loved to make new friends. They continued to talk to their fellow students for fifteen minutes. The bus appeared at 9:05 a.m. Danny and Sam showed the bus driver their student IDs. They sat in the front row, right beside each other as they always did. Sam and Danny had been friends since the third grade. They always protected each other and looked out for each other against bullies and against girls that were no good to them. Danny remembers when he first met Sam very clearly. He remembered during the third grade when he was playing on the slides by himself. Out of nowhere, a ball hit him in the face and he watched as a group of four kids walked over to him and called him short, and a loser. This angered Danny, as he hated when kids like that belittled him. Then one of the kids pushed him on the ground and began to kick him all over his body. Danny felt the blows all over his body as the kids pummeled him; each kick felt more fierce and brutal. Danny began to close his eyes, but out of the corner of his eye, he could see a kid behind them who told them to stop. The kids turned around, laughed, and tried to push him aside. But the kid began to attack them with punches and kicks. Danny could see the kids fight back against the kid defending him. Danny stood on his feet and charged at the four kids. Together they defeated the bullies and they've been friends ever since.

Danny has always been proud of his friend, Sam, ever since he helped him against those bullies. Ever since then, he has always been supportive of Sam and Sam, in turn, has done the same. Danny knew that even though their friendship had been through a lot, this would be their biggest challenge yet. "It's like we're inseparable; we could never be torn apart." Danny thought.

As Danny was in his thoughts, the bus arrived at the school. Danny and Sam got off the bus and walked outside. While Danny was walking, he looked around the school. It was a massive building surrounded by a forest of pure green, humongous trees with a giant football stadium. Danny always enjoyed this school and now, this was his last year. As he continued to walk into the school, he had this feeling in his heart that something wasn't right. Then there was this voice in his head, but it was high pitched like it was from a powerful being. The voice said, "Everything is about to change Danny, everything is about to change."

Chapter 2: Danny Wallace II

Danny and Sam got their schedule from the student office and walked into their first period class. Then Danny saw a tall, African American male with gray hair, a yellow collared shirt, black pants, and black shoes to match. When the man turned around, he had on golden glasses. Danny recognized him immediately; it was his favorite teacher from last year, Mr. Sheppard. His appearance hasn't changed that much and he appeared to have lost some weight from the year before.

Danny walked over to him and said,

"Hello Mr. Sheppard, it's good to see you."

"Good to see you as well Danny. How was your summer?"

"Good, I see that you have changed a little."

"You have as well, you've grown into a fine young man sir."

They shook hands and Mr. Sheppard still had the same tight grip as last year. "He hasn't really changed that much," Danny thought. Just at that moment, Sam walked in.

When he saw them, he said,

"Okay, enough with the love fest you two, it's making me sick."

Mr. Sheppard smiled and said, "I see you haven't changed at all Mr. Samuel; still the class clown."

"Yeah, the same goes to you Mr. Sheppard still picking favorites."

"I'm just having a conversation with one of my students Samuel."

"Yeah, whatever Mr. Sheppard."

Sam takes his backpack off and sits in the front desk. He didn't like being in the front, but he needed to pay attention to the lesson, so he would always sit there. Danny sighed and thought, "Why does Sam still dislike Mr. Sheppard? It seems nothing has changed at all between them." Danny proceeds to sit down right beside

Sam. "He might not be good with teachers, but he is still my best friend," he thought.

Other students walked into the class and sat in the desks. After a few minutes, the class bell rang. Just then another student walked in; she was the most beautiful girl Danny had ever seen. She was African American and her hair was beautifully braided with golden pearls on each end. She had on a black shirt with blue jeans. She walked into the class and Mr. Sheppard introduced her. "Class, I want to introduce you to our new student, Ms. Sonja Morita. She's a senior and she just transferred from Kentridge High School. Let's show her some respect and welcome her with open arms," he said.

Then Sonja sat down next to Danny and introduced herself to him. He shook her hand. Then he noticed a golden necklace around her neck that had an inscription on it. He could tell that the inscription was in Hebrew. Just as before with his amulet, he could feel surge of energy in his brain figuring out what the words mean. In a split second, he knew what the writing meant, it said, "Moses of the Israelites."

"This is going to be interesting," Danny thought. Then suddenly, as Mr. Sheppard was talking about the class rules and syllabus, there was a strange symbol on his arm. It was in the shape of a pyramid with an eye in the middle of it. As well as a strange symbol on the class board. It was a strange number; 666.

"What do these strange symbols mean?" Danny thought.
He also began to wonder why those symbols were there in
the first place—why those specific symbols; what
meaning did they have? Just when Danny was about to
ask Mr. Sheppard a question, the bell rang and everybody
had to go to second period.

Chapter 3: Sam Corbin I

After the bell rang from Mr. Sheppard's class, Sam got up and looked at his schedule. "Thank God," he thought. He never really liked Mr. Sheppard at all and the feeling has always been mutual. Sam saw that his next period class was weight training, located on the first floor in room 105. Sam formed a smirk across his face and took a deep breath showing his sign of relief, finally the class where he was the best at. Despite himself and Danny being best friends since the third grade, the teachers always seemed to respect Danny more than Sam. Not that Sam cared about any of that, of course, but somewhere in the back of his mind, he always wondered why they did so.

"It's not fair that they show more favorable treatment towards Danny than me," he thought. But he would always suppress that thought in the back of his mind as he did not want to compete with his best friend that would make things complicated. While Danny did have the grades, charisma, and a little bit of muscle; it was Sam who excelled in the area of physical fitness. He always had exceptional physical strength. Sam didn't understand the reason, but lifting things for him had always been really easy; even if it was impossible to achieve. He remembered when he was just three years old and he lifted his own bed on top of him. He remembered that his parents and the rest of the family were in a great deal of shock when they saw that tremendous feat of strength shown by a three-year-old boy. Ever since then Sam has been winning weight lifting competitions, one after the other, for years. He continued his train of thought as he began to walk to his weight training class. He went to the first floor and entered room 105. Inside the gym he could clearly see every student inside.

By his count Sam, estimated that there were over thirty students inside the main gym. Sam then had a slight grin on his face. "Now this is a class and I can test my true strength here," he thought. Just then a man walked into the gym leaving everyone silent and facing him as he walked towards the class. Sam could see the man was African American and he had on basketball shorts and a white hood. He also noticed that he looked to be in his mid- forties and had on a golden name tag that said, "Hello my name is Mr. Willis."

Mr. Willis approached the class and in a loud pitched voice said, "Alright boys, my name is Mr. Willis and I will be your coach for weight training class this year. Our first task is to get those muscles of yours flowing with energy. So you all need to get up and jog around the gym for five minutes! Now Go!"

At that moment, everybody except for Sam moaned and started to jog. Sam, on the other hand, just got up and jogged with them. To everybody else this was too hard, but to Sam it felt as if he were home. As he continued to jog, he looked down at his golden chain with words inscribed in Hebrew on that read "Samson the Judge."

The artifact had been in his family for generations. Sam didn't understand why, but he felt as though his family had been connected with Samson of the Bible for a long time. Sam then placed the thought in the back of his mind and focused on jogging.

After ten minutes, Mr. Willis stopped the music and had everybody go to the weight room. Sam looked around and saw that everybody around him that jogged was extremely tired, but for Sam, it felt that he hadn't broken a sweat. It felt natural to him; like it was nothing. With a smirk on his face, he walked over with the rest of the class towards the weight room.

As Sam opened the door of the weight room, he began to look around. The size of the weight room was full of space. The painting color of the weight room was black and red like the colors of the school. All the standard weight equipment was there; the bench press, military press, power clean, and squat machines. Sam then turned to his left and saw there was a collection of dumbbells, as well as posters of ways to work out differently.

Sam then took a seat next to all the other students. He watched and listen as Mr. Willis spoke about the weight room and said,

"All right students, today you're going to learn what type of workout you want to achieve. Whether it's a lean workout or a strength workout, whichever you choose, you have to do your very best at it. Work hard and eventually you will improve yourself and your strength.

Now look at the board and you will see that there are several workout that you can do in order to achieve whatever goals that you have. On the board, there are also sheets that tell you what workout you do and how many sets you have to lift today. Alright, done with the lecture. Go do your workout and get big."

"Yeah!" Responded the entire class.

Sam and all the other classmates went and grabbed the sheets as Mr. Willis instructed. Sam chose the strength work, out of course, he knew that this workout was comfortable and easy for him. Immediately he went to the bench press and started to put forty-five pound weights on each side of the bar, as well as the clips for each weight. He then did three sets of twenty with incredible ease.

Then he added two sets of ten pounds of weights on each side and lifted them.

As he lifted the weights he could feel the muscles in his body growing stronger. He also noticed that the weight felt incredibly light, so he wanted to add more weight. "This feels so easy, I'm not even breaking a sweat," he thought. Then Sam could feel this sudden burst of strength, which gave him the urge to go on and add even more weight. It was as if there was a voice in his head telling him to add more and press forward.

Sam then took of all the weights and added three sets of forty-five pounds of weight on each side of the bar. Sam could also hear other students in the weight room beginning to speak as well as stare at him with shock and awe. Sam heard the students talking. One said,

"Is he really about to lift this weight?"

"I don't know, but my money says he just might," said the other boy.

"No way Josh, that's just impossible. My dad can barely lift that weight and he has been working out for ten years."

Sam then saw that a huge crowd began to form around him as he was about to lift the weight he put on the bench press. Students from every corner of the weight room gathered around him like a pack of wolves. At one point, the crowd got so big and massive that even Mr. Willis took notice and joined the crowd.

Then Sam smiled at the crowd of boys surrounding him. He then lifted the weight and began to feel his muscles in his arms immediately increase in strength. His arms were growing to be massive and with each rep he did with the weight felt lighter and lighter.

As he was lifting, he noticed that students began to take out their phones and cheer Sam on as well as make comments.

"Man the people on Snapchat are going to freak the hell out," said one person.

"Bro, how much more is he going to lift?" replied another student.

"This seems to be impossible."

Sam could then hear the chants,

"Go Sam, hit that weight."

"Yeah Sam, you got this, get it!"

Students continued to record on Snapchat as Sam continued to lift the weight until finally, he stopped. He knew he did sixty reps in all, but to Sam it felt like thirty. Just as Sam stopped lifting, everybody that surrounded him cheered for him, then as the bell rang for third period.

Sam watched as Mr. Willis said,

"Alright students, get to your third period class on time."

"Yes Sir!" the students shouted.

As Sam was about to leave, Mr. Willis stood in front of him and said,

"Hey Sam, can I talk to you for a second?"

"Yeah Mr. Willis, sure, what's up."

"I need to ask you something and I need you to be completely honest with me. Have you been using steroids son?"

Sam smirked, laughed slightly and said, "Mr. Willis, seriously, steroids—I never use steroids sir."

"Then how come you're able to lift that weight? In all my years of body building I have never seen somebody your age be able to lift that type of weight. Hell I've seen men thirty-five years old barely able to lift that weight. How is it that you are able to lift that weight with ease?"

"I can't really explain it to you Mr. Willis. It's just that whenever I lift weight like this it feels natural to me like it's nothing. It's like I'm not even breaking a sweat."

"Well, I'll tell you one thing Sam you have talent with weight lifting. I have a proposal for you. How would you like to compete in a weight lifting competition?"

"I would love to sir."

"Good, the competition begins on March 25th."

Mr. Willis then walked to the board and gave Sam a small flyer of the competition. Then he said,

"I hope to see you there."

Sam smiled and said, "Don't worry I'll be there."

"Good, now get to your third period class son."

"Yes sir."

Sam then smiled and walked towards his third period class. As he walked he began to wonder if he had this mysterious power inside him. "What is this strange feeling of strength?" he thought. Then he pushed the thought aside and ran towards his third period class.

Chapter 4: Danny Wallace III

Danny was passing the blue lockers in the red and black painted hallways of the school. He was heading towards his second period, which was English. His teacher was Ms. Connors, which he knew from last year when she was taught Communications. Danny smiled as Ms. Connors was one of his most favorite teachers at the school. Ms. Connors always had a positive demeanor and personality about her that Danny always enjoyed. As he was in the middle of his thoughts on Ms. Connors, Danny had a thought towards the strange symbols he saw in Mr. Sheppard's room. Whenever Danny wasn't thinking about going to class, the thoughts seemed to pop up in his mind and he wanted to know more. The thoughts of the strange symbols were like an irritating scratch on his back that he just can't reach. Suddenly, he looked up and he saw that he was at the classroom 207. "Guess I'll have to find out about the wierd symbols later," he thought. With anticipation, he walked into the class intending on seeing Ms. Connors, but noticed that she was not in the classroom. "Maybe she is running late," he thought. Danny began to look around the classroom to see that it had some changes compared to last year. The color of the classroom was dark blue and Ms. Connors' desk was in the corner. The desk was made of wood and painted black with a picture of her husband, Keith, and her son, Mitchell, in a gold frame. Danny also noticed that she had posters of several movies that came out this year including Dead Pool, Batman v Superman: Dawn of Justice, and Captain America Civil War. "Guess she's trying to appeal to my generation," he thought.

As Danny continued to explore the classroom, he heard a familiar voice. It said,

"It's been a long time, Danny."

Then Danny turned around and saw a Mexican boy smiling at him. He knew the voice he just heard was extremely familiar. Then with a sudden realization, he immediately knew who the boy in front of him was. It was his extremely close cousin, Luke MonoSol, and judging by his appearance, he has grown significantly. He was wearing blue jeans with black Nike shoes and a green shirt that stated "God Loves" on it. He also had a black beaded cross around his neck and a black hood that matched it. Danny smirked, walked over to his cousin, Luke, and asked,

"Luke, is that you man?"

"It took you that long to remember me?"

"Well, how else was I supposed to recognize you? It's been nine years cousin."

"Yeah, it has primo."

Luke and Danny smirked, then hugged each other, and made a fist bump. Danny smiled. He hadn't seen his cousin Luke since they were nine years old. He remembered that he was always smart and very energetic. Danny remembered that when Luke was nine years old, he was just starting to take Geometry and was able to solve math problems that were extremely difficult with incredible ease. Not only that, but Luke was also able to get straight A's in his class all the time ever since he was in kindergarten. Now that Danny could see his cousin again, there was a since of relief in him knowing that Luke was going to be in this class and that things would be very interesting.

Danny smiled at his cousin as he sat right beside him in the classroom and said,

"Well Luke, I see that you've grown since I last saw you."

"The same can be said for you, Danny." Luke replied.

"Yeah, so have you decided what college you're going to?"

"The University of California comes to mind. By the way you talking to any females yet?"

"No, not really, and it's not always about females you know."

"It's all about the females primo. These girls here are very beautiful and I'm going to get all their phone numbers and the Snapchat."

"Yeah, okay Luke."

"Don't 'okay Luke' me Danny. I always get all the females."

"Really? Then what happen that one time with—"

"Don't even go there, she wasn't worth my time."

Just then Ms. Connors walked in, as well as several other students. Danny looked at his watch and it was 10:00 a.m. "Right on time," Danny thought. As students were getting in their seats, another student walked in and Danny recognized her immediately. It was Sonja Moserita from earlier in Mr. Sheppard's class. When Luke saw her walk in, his mouth was completely open and his eyes got bigger and even bigger. Then Luke said,

"Dang, that girl is fine!"

"Luke, don't try anything, she's mine."

"Yeah right, after class I'm going to get that number."

"Yeah, okay, good luck with that."

Just then the bull rang and Ms. Connors began to talk to all the students about the class.

"Good morning students, how are you all today?" There was a loud groan that followed. Apparently, people were bored already. But Ms. Connors smiled and said, "I figured as much, so instead of having you guys listen to a boring lecture that clearly you don't want to listen to, I'm going to have you guys watch a thirty minute video on English and rhetoric so that you guys have a grasp as to how rhetoric works."

There was a huge smile going across everyone's face in the classroom including Danny's. Ms. Connors smiled then pulled down the board and turned on the projector in the classroom. The video was on YouTube and the title of the video was English Mixed with Rhetoric. In the beginning, everybody in the class seemed to be paying attention, but as the video went on, more and more people began to go on Snapchat and look at their friends' stories and short videos. Other people began to listen to music. It seemed only Danny, Luke, and Sonja were paying attention.

Time seemed to go fast because just when Danny was getting a grasp of rhetoric, the video ended and he smiled knowing that class was over. Ms. Connors told everyone about the homework assignment, which was comparing and contrasting rhetoric. Danny grabbed his bag pack and noticed that Luke was trying to flirt with Sonja, but she didn't like his flirtation at all. Then he watched as Luke said something and in an instant, Sonja slapped Luke in the face then walked out of class.

Danny walked up to Luke and said,

"Luke, what did you say to her?"

"Apparently, she can't take a compliment primo. All I said was that if she worked at Subway then she had nice buns."

Danny smirked and said, "Luke that's not a compliment, that's a pick up line and a horrible one at that."

"Well, it works on other girls."

"I'm surprised that actually works on some of them."

"You'd be surprised how easy it is to flirt with some of these girls primo."

"Okay Luke, well I have to go, see you later cousin."

"Same to you primo."

As Danny left the classroom, he noticed something very strange. The amulet around his neck began to glow and for a brief moment Danny thought he saw a dark cloaked figure standing in the middle of the hallway. But as Danny was walking towards the figure it suddenly disappeared. "What was that? I could have sworn I saw someone or something there," he thought. Then he looked at his amulet and it stopped glowing. Danny walked to his next class.

Far from the English, class a dark figure was standing right next to the side of the school. He was very careful as he didn't want to alert anyone of his presence. His father's orders were to watch out for special teenagers to see if they had united against him but so far, he has found nothing. "Typical humans—always weak and inferior to us," he thought. He was dressed in a black robe with a hood and had a sword inscribed with his name, Azazel, demon of hell. Then he felt a fiery glow behind him and turned around to see it. The fiery glow showed Azazel images of Hell and his master sitting on his throne. He then bowed to his master as he spoke,

"Azazel, have you found the special children yet, have they united?"

"No master, they have not. In fact, they're living normal lives and do not even know of the truth."

"Then perhaps it's time we shake things up for them. Send your followers and hellhounds after them tomorrow."

"Yes, master."

The blazing fiery image stopped, and Azazel disappeared from the school.

Chapter 5: Sam Corbin II

Sam was walking towards the cafeteria with confidence and excitement. After his third and fourth period classes, he rarely had the time to think about Mr. Willis' offer. He couldn't believe that he had been offered a chance to compete in a weight lifting competition. This was what he has been waiting for his entire life. Finally, he had a chance to show off his skills and prove that he is the best at lifting weights. Ever since he was a small boy he felt that weight lifting was his passion. He felt this great power inside him and each time he lifted weights, he could feel it being unleashed. Sam didn't know how to describe it, but it was like energy was expanding throughout his muscles and body as he lifted weights. While Sam was in mid-thought, he could sense that a person was approaching him from behind. He turned around and his best friend Danny was in front of him. Danny was listening to music when he looked up and saw Sam. Sam smiled and said,

"Hey man, how is your day so far?"

"Pretty chill and something very interesting happened in my second period class."

"Like what?"

"I'll tell you after we get our food."

"Alright."

Sam and Danny entered a line of people to get their much needed food. "They had pizza and nachos, so it was bound to be packed." Sam thought. After just a few short minutes, the two friends got their food and sat facing each other at one of the tables beside two soda machines.

Danny broke the silence by continuing the conversation that he and Sam had earlier. He said,

"So back to what I was saying, you know, Luke."

"Your cousin that you haven't seen in nine years?"

"Yeah, that's the one."

"What about him?"

"He's back and he tried to hit flirt with Sonja."

"The one from our first period class? Bro what happened?"

"Let's just say it didn't go well."

Sam could tell when Danny was keeping something from him. He leaned forward and looked Danny right in the eye and said, "Danny, spill it, what happened bro?"

"My cousin, Luke, tried to give a compliment to Sonja that ended up in him being slapped in the face."

"What did he say?"

"He said, 'Hey, Sonja, do you work at Subway cause you have nice buns.'"

Sam and Danny both laughed at the same time. "Luke doesn't have a clue about how to get women at all," he thought, how could he say that comment?" "It's no wonder he got slapped in the face."

Then, just as the two of them were laughing, Sam saw that a Mexican boy and an attractive African American girl were coming towards them. Judging by her braids with golden edges at the end of each one, Sam knew that the girl was Sonja. Sam hadn't seen the Mexican boy before, but he knew it was Danny's cousin, Luke, since the boy appeared to fear Sonja's presence.

Luke and Sonja approached Sam and Danny's table and sat down at the same time, just as Sam and Danny did before only a few minutes ago. "Well, that was a déjà vu moment, he thought. Sam watched as Sonja smiled at both at Danny and Sam and said,

"Hi there Danny and Sam, how are you guys?"

"Good." Sam said.

"Fine." Danny replied.

"Danny, your cousin, Luke, wanted me to come over and talk with you guys."

"Wow Luke, so I take it you're friends with Sonja then."

"Shut up Danny, the slap never happened." Luke replied.

"You know, I'm right here beside you, right?" Sonja stated.

"Yeah, and sorry for the rude pick-up line I gave you earlier."

"Apology accepted. Besides, it was kind of cute, but let's just be friends, okay?"

Sam watched as Luke's cheeks began to turn red blushing at the complement, but also silent due to the fact that he just go friend zoned. Sam spoke to Sonja and said,

"Hey do you like Kentlake High School so far even though it's your first and last year here since you're a senior."

"Yeah, I like it here, my classes are going pretty well and I'm adjusting fairly quickly."

"That's cool."

Sonja then noticed Sam's muscles coming from his biceps. She asked,

"So do you work out a lot?"

"Yeah, in fact my teacher in my weight lifting class gave me a flyer about a weightlifting competition that starts in March."

"That's cool!" Danny and Sonja said at the same time.

"Thanks. But it's that was kind weird with you both of you saying it at the same time. It was cool the first time Danny and I did it, but now it's just getting annoying."

"Sorry Sam, this is the first time I'm hearing of this."

"Well, I was going to tell you until Sonja and Luke came over here."

"Seriously Sam, you're going to blame us for coming over here to sit with you?"

"No I'm just saying that I would have told Danny sooner with no interruptions from you guys and—"

Then Sam paused and when he noticed that Sonja was wearing a golden necklace with a strange inscription on it. He tried to read the inscription on the necklace, but his ability to read was diminished for a moment. Then miraculously, Sam could immediately tell that the inscription read "Moses of the Israelites." Sam didn't know how, but for some reason he knew what the inscription said. Sam could feel it in his head that his brain had made the inscription into words for him to read it with ease. It was if the writing on the necklace was like a puzzle waiting to be solved. He said,

"Hey Sonja, I see the beautiful necklace you have around your neck. Where did you get that?'"

"Oh, my family has had this necklace for generations. It was given to me today by one of my grandparents."

Danny turned towards her and said, "My grandparents did the exact same thing today."

"As did mine." Sam said.

"Mine as well." Luke replied.

Sam wondered what was going on. It can't be a coincidence that all four of them got these golden artifacts at the same time today. As well as the fact that today, all four of them met and in just a few hours, have started to become friends. Sam began to feel as if a plan was at work. He wondered if this was God's plan at work here.

Just as he was in mid-thought the cafeteria bell rang and all students everywhere began to get up and go to their classes. The four of them were no exception. All four of them got up and began to walk.

Then Sam broke the silence and said,

"Hey guys, this has been fun, but I got to go to my fifth period."

"Same here, what class you have?" Luke replied.

"American Government." Sam said.

"Really? Me too." Luke said.

"Same here and I think Sonja has the same class as well."
Danny said.

Sam then held out his schedule along with Danny's,
Luke's, and Sonja's. Sure enough their fifth period was
the same and their teacher was Mr. Gaul.

"Is this the work of God?" Sam thought. He knew deep
down in his heart that this couldn't just be a coincidence.
Sam could feel it in his heart that some divine work was
being done. With that, all four of them walked in unison
as they went to Mr. Gaul's class.

Chapter 6: Danny Wallace IV

Danny walked into his fifth period class along with Sam, Luke, and Sonja. Mr. Gaul was sitting in a chair near his black desk listening to music and didn't seem to notice them coming in. He looked around the classroom smiling as he saw that it looked pretty much the same as last year, with minor changes. There was a picture of the statue of liberty hanging on the wall towards Danny's left that wasn't there last year. Then he looked closely at the picture and noticed that Mr. Gaul, his wife, and two sons were in the picture. The picture was taken on June 12, 2016. Danny smiled at the picture and he turned to see Mr. Gaul still was listening to music with Beats headphones. Danny smirked, then walked over to his teacher and tapped his desk with a loud thump that Mr. Gaul was bound to hear. It succeeded and he looked up at Danny and smiled. He said,

"Mr. Wallace, it's good to see you. How's your senior year going?"

"Pretty good. I like all of my classes so far."

"That's good and I see you and Sam are still friends."

"Yeah, he's cool."

"You know I can hear you guys talking right?" Sam said, as he was sitting at a desk in the front.

"Don't worry Sam, we're only talking good things about you." Danny replied.

"Alright, I better not hear any bad things about me."

Danny smiled then turned to Mr. Gaul and said,

"Well, it's good to see you Mr. Gaul."

"Same goes to you Mr. Wallace."

Just then the bell rang and more students started to come in and sit in the desks. As the students continued to come in for what seemed like that of a huge wave, Mr. Gaul smiled. He always liked big classes because he felt he could reach the heart of more students while educating them on the past.

After five minutes the bell rang again signifying that class was about to start. Everybody was in their seats talking. Mr. Gaul got up and told everybody to take out their headphones so he could talk. They looked at him for a second then put away their headphones with the intention on listening to him. Mr. Gaul said,

"Alright class, today we are going to begin to learn about how the government works. In order to do that, we are going to learn about the founding fathers and how our government came to be. One of the things we are also going to learn about is our structure of government and the three branches of government; the legislative, executive, and judicial branches. So without further interruptions, I have a PowerPoint that I want to present to you that starts off with a video. Now, let us begin."

Mr. Gaul turned on the projector above the students then connected a cord to his computer. The video began to play and it was on the History Channel's website discussing the founding fathers of America. While the video began to play, Danny began to pay attention to the video and take notes. But after a few short sentences, he suddenly stopped, slowly put his pencil down and closed his notebook. He then began to think.

Danny began to have a strange feeling deep within his heart. "Why am I even studying about the American Government?" he thought. "What has it done for me and more importantly what has it done for African Americans. This system of government, the so called "land of the free" has done nothing more than keep African Americans down from slavery, to Jim Crow, the KKK, and now police brutality. This free system has kept African

Americans down for far too long. Yet I'm learning about a system that was created by a bunch of slaver owners." The American system was hypocritical in his eyes and frankly he was getting sick of constantly learning about the system. Danny began to realize that this feeling inside him was not anything new to him at all. Rather, it was just all the anger he had for this system was now coming to the surface. Anger—that's what it boiled down to in his eyes. Anger at this system, anger at the way it has treated his people like animals and second class citizens, and anger at how police constantly kill unarmed black males as if they were trash.

As he was in mid-thought, he noticed that the pencil he had in his hand began to break in half. He also noticed that he was breathing very heavily. Sam noticed and said,

"Hey Danny, calm down. I feel it too, but now it's not the time."

Danny then calmed down and slowed his breathing down to a normal pace. He appreciated Sam calming him down. But he was wrong about one thing; now is exactly the time to be angry. How can he learn about a system that has suppressed his people? Danny then thought that if he could learn all about the system of American Government he might just be able to change it one day. Danny swore from then on that he would learn everything he could from this class then make the system anew.

Just as Danny was in thought, the video ended and Mr. Gaul began to lecture the class on the government through the PowerPoint. The lecture seemed like a blur to Danny as he didn't really want to learn about the hypocritical system, but he was forced to; at least that is what he felt like. Then he reached into his backpack and grabbed another pencil and started to take notes in his notebook. As Mr. Gaul continued to lecture on the lesson, Danny took notes in critical detail. Danny would write down the information on every slide in his notebook like his life depended on it.

After what seemed like a blur, the bell rang and the class suddenly ended. Danny then got up along with Sam,

Luke, and Sonja. Mr. Gaul said goodbye to his students and they left the class.

❖ _____

_____

Danny walked out of his sixth period class, Spanish, early due to the fact that all they had gotten was a syllabus and talked about the conjunctions of estar and ser. But with his cousin, Luke, in the class helping him, everything seemed to be easy. The class was thirty minutes, but to Danny it seemed like five minutes. Luke had always helped Danny when it came to Spanish simply because they were family and he had always wanted to speak in Spanish more fluently. Then Danny walked over to the buses where Sam was waiting for him and together they walked onto their specific bus, showed their IDs and sat in the front rows beside each other.

After the bus start moving, Danny's thoughts were completely on the strange symbols he saw in Mr. Sheppard's classroom earlier. The pyramid with the eye in the middle of it, as well and the number 666 on his arm, made Danny wonder what those symbols meant. Ever since he saw those symbols, throughout the day he had constantly been thinking about them. It seems the symbols never escaped his head. He felt something deep in his heart telling him that he needed to find out what those symbols mean. As he was in mid thought Sam said,

"Hey Danny, did you notice anything that seemed to be off today?"

"Yeah, why?" he replied.

"Well, I noticed several things that seemed to be too coincidental. Like the fact that your cousin shows up at this school after nine years and the fact that Sonja came here to this school. Also, the fact that all four of us have these strange amulets given to us from our grandparents on the same day." Sam replied.

Then Danny thought about it. Sam was right, it did seem to be too coincidental that Sonja just transferred here today and that she happens to have an amulet in Hebrew like his. As well as his cousin, Luke, returning did seem to be questionable. He said,

"Yeah and I also noticed that, as well as some strange symbols in Mr. Sheppard's room today. There was a pyramid with an eye in the middle of it, as well as the number 666 on his arm and I don't know what those symbols mean, but I intended to find out."

Sam smiled and said "I guess great minds think alike."

"I guess so. Hey, do you like Sonja?"

"Maybe, she is kind of cute, why?"

"Maybe I'll put you on her."

"Nah bro, I can handle this myself."

"Okay cool, good luck bro."

"Thanks man."

Danny and Sam continued to talk until the bus arrived at their bus stop. Then the two of them got off and said,

"Bye Danny, see you tomorrow."

"The same goes to you Sam."

As Danny was walking back to his house, his mind was continuously thinking about the strange symbols in Mr. Sheppard's room. "At this point, these thoughts seem endless." he thought. It was as if something was telling him deep inside that he should learn about those symbols; they hold some type of significance in a grand scheme. Danny could feel the mysterious voice in his head like a whisper, it said, "Find out you must find out." Danny immediately ran towards his home and opened the door.

He felt that he knew what he had to do. He ran towards his room, closed the door with a little force, and turned on his computer. He started to type the strange symbols into Google and what he found shocked him.

There were several pictures of a secret organization known to many as the Illuminati and the strange symbols that he saw in Mr. Sheppard's room were a part of their symbols in the organization. After looking through countless websites about them from conspiracy theories to actual historical facts on how the organization was created, Danny was overwhelmed with astonishment that an organization like this could exist. While there were many conspiracies about the Illuminati, one very prominent one is that they are going to take over the world using a One World Government or what many people dub it as the New World Order.

There were also several conspiracies on who the Illuminati leader is. Some people say it's Pope Francis, leader of the Catholic Church. Others say that former President Obama was the antichrist worshipping demons. Danny felt the need to take a break from his research. He was getting much information at one time that he needed to process it. He could also feel that his eyes grew tired and immediately went to his bed to take a quick nap. As he put his head on his black and orange pillow, he closed his eyes; to finally sleep and began to dream.

Danny awoke and he looked around as he saw people form into a huge crowd. Judging by the way they are looking behind him in shock and awe, he knew that some type of event had taken place. He slowly turned around to see a man on a wooden cross and with a crown of thorns on his head. Danny recognized the man as Jesus Christ, or more correctly in his original Hebrew name Yeshua, the Savior of the world. Danny looked on as the crowd of people where moaning and weeping over the death of their Messiah. Then the crowd turned to see a man in battle armor approach Jesus with a spear in his hands. Danny saw an inscription on the armor that said "Longinus." He watched as Longinus went over to Jesus and pierced his spear into Jesus' side. There was shock and awe in the crowd of people. Especially in the group of twelve standing side by side wailing and crying, and they were powerless to do anything. Danny recognized the twelve as the twelve disciples of Jesus.

Then the scene completely shifts and Danny looks up at the moon beaming on him. He began to look around and he saw flags being waved on each side. "This must be a battlefield," he thought. He looked to his left and he could see an army of knights with a flag having a cross on it in the background. Danny then turned to his right and ahead of him was an army of people with turbans on their heads and the Islamic crest on their breast plates. In the background, there was the temple of Jerusalem, but it had the Islamic crest flag over it. Danny watched and the two armies charged at each other yelling and screaming, riding on their horses as they came closer and closer until both armies clashed. Swords clashed with one another and on both sides blood was being shed as the two sides plunged their weapons into each other. As the carnage continued, Danny could see, in the distance, a group of nine knights riding into the battle. They were riding on black horses with a red cross on the breast plates of their knight uniforms. Danny watched as the knights rode into the epic battle killing all of the Islamic knights and helping the Christian army capture Jerusalem.

After the battle is won, the scene moves on to were the nine knights that Danny saw earlier are in an underground tunnel with candles clearly looking for something. Then they see a bright glow and they head toward it. The object is emitting a glow that is revealed to be a spear. Danny recognized it as the spear he saw earlier during the crucifixion of Jesus. Then Danny watches as a hole of light opens and he walks through it.

Danny looks around to see a fiery place filled with lava and crispy landscape, as well as people burning in pain and agony. Danny begins to walk around and see creatures with horns on their heads and black eyes heading towards a winged figure sitting on a chair that appears to be his throne. The winged figure has black wings and a scar across his right eye. Then he got up and said,

"Hello my children. After one hundred thousand years of being imprisoned here for rebelling against my father, the time has come and soon the first of the seals will be broken. My favorite demon, Azazel, is gathering his followers as we speak and sooner or later they will find the Spear and break the first seal. When that happens, we will be one step closer to waging war against humanity and reclaim our birthright and achieve Victory!"

"Yeah!" said the crowd of demons.

"Now chant my name, so that it will lead us to victory."

"All hail The Evil One." chanted the crowd.

The crowd of demons chanted The Evil One for a long time before Danny looked around and he could see that he was on a mountain top. Danny could then hear a loud pitched voice. It said,

"Danny Wallace, you must find the others like you. I have given each of you special abilities to stop the dark forces. You must lead the others and find a special artifact."

Danny looked up to the sky and said, "I will, but who are you?"

The voice said, "I am that I am."

Suddenly Danny recognized the voice. It had always been with him whenever he needed guidance. It had been inside him giving him advice and helping him with his fast reflexes. He knew what the voice was, he then said, "God." Then Danny woke up as his alarm went off and he got up. He wondered if it was a dream or was it real. Still thinking about it, he gets up and starts to get ready for school.

Chapter 7: The Descendants Assemble!

Danny was right beside Sam in the front row of the bus just like always on the way to school. But Danny couldn't shake the feeling that there was something off today. It has been a day since he had those strange dreams. Ever since the dream he had last night the feeling has never escaped him. He remembered it all too well; the images of the Longinus piercing Jesus Christ's side and the nine knights finding the Spear in Jerusalem, as well as the demons of Hell, and a mysterious creature called the Evil One talking to his demons preparing for a war with humanity and bringing about the end of the world. These thoughts made Danny very cautious. It was as if he was shaken with fear and anticipation of what's to come.

"What if the dream was real?" Danny thought. It felt so real and vivid the way the images were seen. When he told Sam about the dreams, he explained that he had the same dream last night and that they weren't real. But Danny felt otherwise. Ever since he saw those visions, especially the one on the mountain top were he talks to God, he wonders if he will find Luke and Sonja in order to tell them about the mission to stop the Dark Ones.

As soon as he got off the, bus Danny instantly heard the high pitched voice of God in his head telling him, "Everything is about to change Danny Wallace. Everything will change for the rest of your life." Then the mysterious voice disappeared again. Danny watched as Sam looked at him. He waved to signal that he was fine and both of them continued to walk towards the school.

As they walked inside the school, Danny could feel that someone was watching him and slowly walking behind him. He then turned around and saw that it was his cousin, Luke. Once he saw Luke and Sam, Danny knew he had to tell them about the visions he saw last night. With haste he walked up to them and he said,

"Hey guys I have something to tell you."

"What is it?" Luke and Sam said sim

 "Okay I know this is going to sound crazy, but I have been having these weird dreams. In the dreams I see Jesus

Christ being impaled by a spear and later seeing that same spear being discovered by Knights. I also see a mysterious creature called The Evil One in Hell gathering his demons and preparing for war against us. At the end of my dream I am on a mountain top and a powerful voice telling me to find others like myself to stop these Dark Forces."

"Well Danny why are you telling us this." Sam said

"Because I think you guys are like me, we have special powers. I also believe we are in grave danger and we need to find Sonja. She could be one of us."

"Man, that's crazy there's no way this could be true." Sam said.

"Well it does seem possible given the fact that we all have these artifacts in our possession." Luke said

"Yeah and I'm not going to lie does make sense now that I think about it." Sam said

"Guys there is no time to waste we have to find Sonja. We need to move now."

As the three of them walked into the school and near the hallways, the three of them heard a loud howl behind them. All three of them turned around at the same time and they could see a creature with black fur and red eyes with small horns attached to it. It was as big as a grizzly bear, but had the eyes of pure evil. Danny didn't know who this creature was, but he knew that it was dangerous.

He then turned to Luke and Sam and said, "I think it's time to Run!"

"Yeah, let's bail!" Sam replied.

All three of them began to run as fast as they could with the hellhound lunging towards them growling and chasing after them.

Chapter 8: The Descendants Assemble

II

Danny, Luke, and Sam began to run so fast that they seemed to be sprinting across the hallways away from the mysterious creature chasing them. Danny was leading ahead of Luke and Sam. He turned around and to his horror, saw that the creature was inches away from mauling his cousin and best friend. He knew that he couldn't just let his cousin and best friend die right in front of him. So, he reached out his hand and miraculously, the creature stopped running in its tracks. It was as if the creature was forcibly stopped by his hand. Danny could feel a strange power growing inside him. He pushed his hand towards the creature and watched as it was pushed towards the wall. Danny looked at his hand wondering what this mysterious power was. He had never felt such power in his life. He could still feel the energy inside him, like it was flowing through his entire body. "What kind of power is this?" he thought, "What else can I do with this new power?" As he was in mid-thought, Sam and Luke caught up to him and said,

"Danny, that was unbelievable! How did you do that?" Sam said.

"Yeah primo, it was pretty impressive." Luke said.

Danny looked towards them in shock and awe and said, "I don't know guys I just felt the energy flowing through me and it just happened, I can't describe it. It was truly amazing. But guys, we need to continue to look for Sonja."

"I think it would be a better idea if we split up to find her that way, we can cover more ground." Luke said.

Danny nodded agreeing with Luke's idea and said,

"I agree Luke, see if you can cover more ground, Sam and I are going to find Sonja."

Luke smiled as he turned around and ran towards the opposite direction near the knocked-out creature.

Danny looked at Sam and said,

"Hey, let's go find Sonja."

"I'm right behind you."

Suddenly, the first period starting bell rang. Danny and Sam looked at each other. If they were going to find Sonja, what better place than first period classroom?

❖--

At the beginning of first period Sonja was reading a book in Mr. Sheppard's class. She listened as he was giving her a lecture on the Crusades, but she knew most of the information that was being given. Mr. Sheppard took notice of that while giving his lecture, but he did nothing but smile. Sonja then thought, "I guess he likes that I'm multitasking." As she looked at the clock, she realized that class was almost over and that Mr. Sheppard would eventually stop talking. After a few more minutes of Mr.

Sheppard's unbearable lecture, the bell finally rang ending first period. All at once everybody got up and started to go their second period class. Mr. Sheppard then walked over to Sonja as she stood up getting ready to leave and stated he needed to talk to her. He then went over to his door, closed it, and with a small click, locked the door. Mr. Sheppard turned around with a huge grin on his face and said,

"Now Sonja, I'm going to ask you a question and I need you to tell me the truth okay."

"Sure, what do you want to know?"

Sonja then looked around the class and noticed that Mr. Sheppard had strange symbols in his room. One of them was a pyramid with an eye in the middle of it and she noticed his arm; he had a mark of the number 666. Immediately after she noticed the mark, she realized that something was wrong and that something bad was about to happen. As Mr. Sheppard approached her he said

"Sonja, where is it? Where is the Spear of Destiny?"

Sonja was in complete shock said, "Look Mr. Sheppard, sorry to burst your bubble, but I have no idea what the Spear of Destiny is and even if I did, I would never tell you where it is."

"Look don't play dumb with me I know you have it!."

"As I stated before, I have no idea what you are talking about."

"Well it seems that you have forced me to take drastic *measures*!"

Mr. Sheppard quickly turned around holding a red and black colored dagger with a golden blade and lunged at Sonja, intending on stabbing her eye. She ducked underneath the blade, barely dodging the attack, quickly used her leg to trip Mr. Sheppard. Then she tried to punch him the face, but before she could deliver the blow, he kicked her in the face sending her back to land on a desk. Sonja could feel a spark of power inside her and she looked towards her hand. Suddenly, with a flash of white light, a golden tilted dagger appeared in her hand. Then at the same, time both Sonja and Mr. Sheppard did a front flip and charged at each other. Mr. Sheppard went for

Sonja's shoulder, but she grabbed his hand to block the attack. Then with her dagger in hand, plunged the blade into Mr. Sheppard's eye, causing him to scream in pain. Then she did a front flip and kicked his face, causing him to fly all the way back to the board and pass out.

Just then, Danny and Sam busted open the door with looks of surprise on their faces, as Mr. Sheppard was out and Sonja was standing tall in triumph.

Sonja was in complete shock at what she just did said "Guys what's going on?"

Danny said "Well, it's a long story but basically we have been called by God to stop the Evil One from taking over the world"

"Well who is the Evil One?"

"I don't know but if you come with us, we can find out together."

Sonja was at first hesitant as this sounded crazy but given the circumstances, she realized that this must be true. She then joined both Danny and Sam. All three of them left the classroom. Sonja then noticed that Danny's cousin was missing she then asked

"Hey guys where is Luke?

❖ --

Luke was wondering through the hallway looking around for other weird creatures. After the first encounter with one of those things, he couldn't take any more chances of being surprised. He kept walking straight when out of nowhere, two red cloaked figures appeared in front of him side by side. Luke stood completely still and took a moment to analyze their appearance. Each of them had on the weird symbols of a pyramid with an eye in the middle, as well as black and red wooden sticks that appeared in their hands. Luke had a chance to look at their eyes and he could see that their pupils were pure red, as if it were a sign of their intense rage that filled them.

Suddenly, with a deep tone in their voice, both men said,

"Give us the location of the Spear Luke MonoSol."

"I don't know where it is. By the way you guys both look weird."

Luke then suddenly felt this strange power flowing within him. He opened his eyes began to see electricity flowing across his body. Without hesitation, Luke quickly charged towards the two men. The first guy attempted to punch him in the face, but Luke knew the attack was coming and dodged it, sideswiped the man, then reached out his hand to the second figure and caused him to be sent a blast of electricity causing him to be send flying against the wall. The first cloaked figure then tried to punch Luke again, but this time went for his stomach. Before the punch could even make impact Luke grabbed the cloaked figure's bald fist and delivered an elbow to the side of his head causing him to be stunned. Then Luke did an arm drag and as the cloaked figure was slammed to the ground he kicked him in the face knocking him out. Suddenly, he heard footsteps approaching and he instantly turned around ready to fight, but he could only see that it was his cousin Danny with Sam and Sonja.

Danny then smiled and said " Well that was easy."

Chapter 9: The Quest for the Spear Begins

Danny smiled at his cousin, Luke, but at the same time was surprised that he was able to unlock his abilities so quickly. Since the two red cloaked Illuminati followers are knocked out completely, it seems Luke is a pretty skilled fighter, or at least he mastered the skills of fighting and using his powers at the same time. He looked around and saw that all four of them were standing in the hallway and realized something.

"Guys we need to figure out what this Spear is and why is it important that these crazy guys want to find it so badly."

"I agree. We need to go to the library for information." Luke said

Suddenly, all four of them heard the loud pitched voice of God ringing in their ears, causing them to cover their ears.

God said,

"Now that the four of you have united, you now are drawn to each other. The four of you shall be called "The Descendants" because you are descendants of my chosen. I will now give you weapons that are unique to each of you.

Suddenly, a white flash of light appeared before the group and each member was given a specific weapon. Sonja was given a staff and on it there was an inscription in Hebrew that read "The Staff of Moses." Sam was given a blade

that had the appearance of a jawbone of an animal and on

it read "The Jawbone of Samson." Danny was given two

golden swords with a black metal blades and on each

blade it read "The Swords of David the Warrior." Luke

was given a sword that read "The Sword of Solomon."

Then the voice of God said "Now that you have the tools

needed to defeat your enemies, your task is clear. Go and

remember that my spirit will always be in you. Draw on it

for strength and power."

Then the voice of the Almighty disappeared once more.

After taking a moment to recover, Luke said, "Guess

that's all the motivation we need." The four of them, now

known as the Descendants, proceed to walk towards the library and gather information of the Spear.

Luke went towards a computer and after a few minutes of looking up information about the strange symbols he saw and the spear those guys kept talking about, he said,

"Well guys I think I know what group Mr. Sheppard and those guys belong to. There called the Illuminati and the artifact they are after is the Spear of Destiny. There are many legends about it. Some say that it can bring people back to life while others say it's a weapon of great power. As it turns out, the Spear of Destiny is a spear used by a Roman solider named Longinus, who used his spear to pierce Jesus Christ on the cross. The legend goes that whoever controls the Spear controls the world. A weapon like that with unlimited power—the Illuminati could do anything with that object."

Luke, is the Spear in one piece?" Sonja asked.

"Unfortunately, no Sonja. Many have searched for the Spear to obtain its divine power. According to many websites the Spear split into three pieces across the world in hopes of it being never united."

"How did the Spear get split in the first place?" Sam asked.

Luke responded, "Well, like I said before, many groups over the centuries have searched for the Spear. According to conspiracy websites Adolf Hitler tried to use the

Spear's Power but failed and as a result lost World War II."

"Luke, do you have any idea where the Spear could be now?" Danny asked.

"We could try looking for one of the soldiers during WWII that found the Spear, or we could try looking for the three possible locations ourselves." Luke replied.

"I would suggest we look for the one of the allied soldiers. If he is still alive, he would probably be in his eighties and at his house, Luke can you search for retired veterans living in a housing complex?" Sonja asked.

Luke looked on Google for the nearest hospital and after a few seconds found one.

"The closest housing complex is University Square Senior Housing. It's about fifteen minutes from here and the only veteran living there is Chris Matthews."

"You have the address?" Sonja asked.

"Yes."

"Then let's go!"

It took exactly fifteen minutes to get to the housing complex by car. Luke was the only one that could drive among the group and he had a 1985 Corvette that his father gave him. After fifteen of driving and getting food along the way, the group got to the comples. When they entered the building, Luke walked over to the nurse taking care of Chris Matthews and said,

"Is Chris Matthews, the WWII veteran here we need to talk with him."

"Yes, of course, he's in his room I'll be glad to take you to room."

"Thank you." Luke replied.

All four of them walked down to his room 109. But something was wrong, the door was already opened. Luke then opened the door only to find a gun pointed at his head by an elderly man. He was barely holding a shot gun pointing at them when he said, "Walk in the door slowly, lock it, and hands where I can see them!"

Luke and the others did what he said and locked the door. Then all four of them had their hands up.

Then Luke said, "Chris Matthews, we're not here to hurt you."

"How do I know you not with those strange cult people with pyramid symbols on them, looking some mystical spear?"

"Because if we were with him, you would be dead by now, but were not killers. My name is Luke and the others are Danny, Sonja, and Sam."

"Show me your weapons!" Chris Matthews replied.

One by one they all took out their weapons and showed them to Chris, who was amazed by them. Then he said,

"You're the special children, aren't you?"

"How do you know that were special?" Danny replied.

"Because back when me and my fellow comrades discovered the Spear of Destiny in Austria, Hungary, an angel of the Lord appeared to us. He told us to split the spear into three pieces and that one day, four special children would join together to find the Spear to stop a great evil. After the war, my friends Jake and Robert took the Spear and split it up in three pieces and scattered them across the globe. The first piece is in the Eiffel Tower in Paris. The second is in the Great Wall of China and the last piece is in Jerusalem. But beware, there all enemies everywhere so watch your back and be on guard."

"Thanks Chris, for helping us."

"No problem and may God bless you all. To show you all my support, take my shotgun Luke, you might need it."

"Thanks." Luke replied.

Luke was about to shake the man's hand when suddenly, an arrow went right through his chest. Chris gasped for air and immediately fell down to the floor. Then Luke looked out the window to see a black hooded figure with Illuminati symbols and a bow and arrow on top of another house across from them. The figure then aimed his arrow at Luke, ready to fire. Just as he shot his arrow at Luke, he could feel someone pull his head back into the room. Luke turned to see that it was his cousin Danny, who said,

"Hey, we need to leave now!"

"Yeah, let's go." Luke replied.

Danny and Luke, accompanied by Sonja and Sam, all grabbed their weapons from God and left the room. Just as they started to run, they spotted four black and red cloaked figures with red eyes and black swords. Luke said,

"Guys, we don't have time for this."

"Give us the location of the Spear's pieces or else!"

"You'll have to catch us first!" Danny replied.

Then Danny reached out his hand and all four of the red cloaked figures were suddenly behind him several feet, he suddenly realized that he could that he could teleport.

Sam noticed this too smiled as he punched the ground, causing the floor to crack around their enemies causing them to fall into the ground below. Luke then grabbed Sam and Sonja and used his super speed to run towards Danny. The group quickly left the house. They saw Luke's Corvette and with haste, got into the car and starting driving. The Illuminati followers were right behind them. They all watched as the summoned four hellhounds after them. Sam looked around and said

"Danny, we need a way out of here!"

"Don't worry I got this!"

Danny then grabbed his door and concentrated on the location of the first piece of the Spear in Paris. . He then concentrated on teleporting by focusing on imagery of Paris such as the Eiffel tower and in an instant all four of them were in the city in Luke's car. If they were going to find the three pieces to the Spear of Destiny, Paris would be a place to start.

Chapter 10: The Plan of Attack and Search for the First Piece

Sam was beside his best friend, Danny, and they were accompanied by Sonja and Luke as they were walking in Paris blending in with the crowd. All four of them were discussing how they're going to find the first piece of the legendary Spear of Destiny. Luke began the discussion.

"So when we find the first piece, how are we going to deal with the opposing forces of the Illuminati? I mean, they're bound to come find us as well."

"We deal with them by fighting them head on just like we did at the school!" Sam replied.

"But we have to have a strategy, Sam, we can't just charge at them guns blazing. There needs to be a plan." Luke responded.

"Luke's right, Sam, if we go in there and attack them head on, we are most likely going to get ourselves killed. The only reason we were able to defeat the Illuminati followers last time was because they underestimated us. They won't make the same mistake twice. They'll be expecting us to be in Paris and fight. But if we play our cards right, we can defeat them and get the first piece of the Spear." Danny replied.

"That's easier said than done. What makes you think the Illuminati will be easily fooled by us? Not to that the Illuminati is being controlled by a mysterious creature called the Evil One. We can't take him lightly." Sonja stated.

"Man, I can't stand the Illuminati. If I see them again, I'm taking them all down." Sam said.

"No Sam, we can't do that. We have to come together as a team to take them on." Luke said.

"Well Luke, I work better alone and I have been chosen by God!" Sam replied.

"Well Sam, if you haven't noticed, all four of us are chosen by God and we are all tasked by him to stop The Evil One. So, like I said before, were going to have to work together here as a team if we want to defeat the Illuminati." Luke angrily stated.

Sam gives a frown on his face and sucks his teeth, annoyed with Luke's comments. This confirms why he doesn't work in a group and prefers to do everything on his own. It's because of people like Luke who feel that they know everything. When he is by himself, he feels like he is in control and he can only work with Danny because they're best friends and they get along so well.

As the team was thinking about their plan of attack against the Illuminati they continued to search for the Spear in Paris.

As they continued to walk through the city all four of them were surprised by the way it looked compared to the United States. They were in complete amazement by the sights and the sounds of the place. The streets and even the buildings looked completely different. The weather was hot, so Danny was sweating like crazy. But at the same time everybody knew why they were there; to find the first piece of the Spear of Destiny. If they could figure out how to navigate the city, of course. Immediately, Danny said

"Okay guys, any idea on finding the first piece to the Spear of Destiny in this vast city of Paris?"

"I think we should get a map of the city and go from there." Luke replied.

"Yeah, but that could take a while" Sam said.

"Well, we have time, plus it's going to be fun to check out the city of love." Sonja said.

"Of course, you're going to say something like that Sonja." Luke said.

"Yeah, I happen to enjoy this place already, plus it will give us a chance to explore the city." Sonja replied.

"Sonja, can you focus? We're here to find a piece of the most powerful artifact in the world not be tourist." Luke replied.

"Can't we do both?"

"Both of you shut up. We all know what we have to do, now let's check out the city of Paris, find the first piece of the Spear and get out." Danny said.

"And if the Illuminati come after us again, we'll kick their butts like the last time or I will at least and I'll have some fun doing it." Sam said.

With the mission clear, all four Descendants walked together as a group searching for the piece of the prized artifact. As they were walking, someone was watching them from a distance with binoculars. It was none other than the Illuminati ready to attack if necessary.

❖ --

Danny was walking along with Luke to look for a map of Paris. Danny and Luke thought that by finding a map of the city they could find the piece of the spear quicker.

While Sonja and Sam wanted to look for the piece of the Spear elsewhere. The two of them decided that they wanted to cover more ground by splitting up, but Danny and Luke knew that Sonja just wanted to check out the city. Danny was at a coffee shop listening to music when Luke showed up and said,

"Hey, I found a map of Paris. It actually was that hard to find."

"Seems like you were surprised by that." Danny said.

"I was, I mean, I didn't expect to find a map of Paris that easily given that fact that we've only been here for about ten minutes."

"Maybe if we look for the Eiffel Tower and find the piece of the spear there."

After Danny and Luke looked through the map of Paris they were able to find the Eiffel tower. Luke then said

"Wow primo that was easy. I think we need to take a break let's go to the church close by to rest it's hot out here!"

"I agree."

Danny got up from the coffee shop and followed Luke. After five minute walk, they both saw a large church and entered. The inside of the church was massive. It had over twenty rows of seats with paintings of angels all across the windows of the church. There was one particular painting that interested Danny and Luke. It was a depiction of an angel in battle armor wielding a sword, stabbing a horned figure. As they looked closely at the painting a voice behind them said, "That's the archangel, Michael."

At the same time Danny and Luke turned around to see a man standing in front of them. He had on a black outfit with a white bow tie. At his left side Danny could see a golden name tag that said, "Father Richards." Luke said,

"Hi Father Richards. My name is Luke, and this is my cousin Danny. We came here to cool off from the outside heat when we saw that really spectacular painting and you said that was the archangel Michael."

"That's right. The depiction is describing a period during the war in heaven when Michael defeats Satan in battle." Father Richards replied.

"Wow, that's really cool. Tell me Father Richards, are there more archangels than just Michael?"

"Yes, there are Luke. In fact there are two more archangels besides Michael, and they are Gabriel and Raphael. You can include Satan because he was once called Lucifer once he was God's most favorite archangel, but ever since his fall from grace they are the only ones now that stand beside Michael and God in heaven."

"Hi Father Richards, I'm Danny and I was wondering what does the word archangel mean?"

"Good question Danny. The word archangel comes from the Greek which means chief angel. The four archangels are a supreme breed of angels and have command over the rest of the heavenly host. They are fierce, powerful warriors for God and they are also his messengers. The archangel Gabriel is considered to be God's greatest messenger." Father Richards replied.

"Thank you, Father. My cousin Luke and I would like to rest now."

"Of course, gentleman, I will leave you to it. If you have any other questions just ask me."

Father Richards walked away from Danny and Luke. As he does so, both Danny and Luke sit down in chairs and begin to rest. As they both rested, they experience visions of Sam and Sonja in danger fighting off the Illuminati and Sonja being captured. At the same time, both Danny and Luke immediately stop resting and turn to each other.

"Sam and Sonja need our help." Luke said.

"Yeah, I know, we have to save them." Danny replied.

They both thank Father Richards for everything and leave the church.

Sam and Sonja were at a restaurant eating. Sonja seemed to love the city of Paris so far while Sam seemed annoyed by it. They went continued walking saw the Eiffel Tower, so that way they would come back a get the piece of the Spear. But not before they eat though. After they are done eating, they go back to the Eiffel Tower and as they move close to it, both of their artifacts on them seemed to glow at the same time. It was as if they could sense the piece of the Spear. Once there, practically beneath the tower they both look for the Spear.

After searching for five minutes both Sonja and Sam find nothing. "Where is that first piece?" Sam shouted. Then out of the corner of her eye, Sonja sees a brown scroll in one of the Tower's metal pieces above them. She points to it and Sam gives her a boast to help her. Sonja grabs the scroll and inside it is a black staff with golden ends to each side. A thunder cloud suddenly appears once Sam grabs the staff.

"This must be the first piece. We did it Sonja." Sam said.

"Thanks for making this easier for me Descendants," said a strange voice.

Sam and Sonja both turn around and see large cloaked creature that seemed to be with red eyes and a flaming sword that was inscribed. The mysterious figure also had twenty Illuminati soldiers behind him.

"Who are you?" Sam asked

"My name is Azazel child. I have come for that piece of the Spear. My master demands it."

"Well Azazel if you want the piece of the spear your going to have to take it from us!" Sam said

"No problem." Azazel replied.

Then Azazel pointed his finger and said, "Attack them!"

And with that, all of the Illuminati followers charge at the two of them.

Chapter 11: The Confrontation

Danny and Luke were running through the city of Paris as fast as they could. The both of them were in using their respective powers of teleportation and super speed as well jumping over objects and pushing by people heading towards the Eiffel Tower. Each of their faces showing concern about their friends Sonja and Sam. Danny was thinking about Sam a lot. He was his best friend and he wasn't going to stand by as his friend fought off waves of Illuminati followers alone. As they moved closer to the Eiffel Tower, they continued to experience visions of Sam and Sonja fighting off Azazel and keeping the piece of the artifact with them.

Danny turned to Luke and said, "We have to find them and stop the Illuminati before it's too late."

"Yeah, I know I just hope we can make it in time." Luke replied.

They continued to run towards the Eiffel Tower as fast as they could, knowing what dangers that were ahead of them. As the Illuminati followers were charging at Sam and Sonja, Sonja turned to Sam and said,

"What do we do?"

"We fight and don't worry we can take them on." Sam replied.

"There's twenty of them and two of us."

"Hey, don't tell me about the odds okay. With our combined powers we should be able to take these guys down."

Together, both Sam and Sonja charged at the Illuminati followers and began to fight them. As they got surrounded by them, Sam and Sonja went back to back as they were battling the Illuminati followers of Azazel underneath the Eiffel Tower. Sonja was using the Staff of Moses to create a powerful blast of light against the enemy forces, while Sam was using his super strength to defeat the followers with ease. One by one, Sam was grabbing the red hooded figures and punching them in the face with devastating effects on them.

Both Sam and Sonja were surprised at how effective they both were working as a team. As Sam was continuing to battle the army of Illuminati followers, he felt a jolt of excitement like he never felt before. To him, there was this sudden thrill of battle that he felt every time he fought the followers of Azazel. With each blow, he was delivering to them he could feel himself getting stronger and more powerful. "So, this is what real combat feels like." he thought, as he continued to fight and enjoy battle. Sam then turned to Sonja as she kicked a hooded figure in the face and at the same time, hitting another one with the Staff of Moses. She then took the legendary staff and slammed it to the ground, creating a powerful shockwave against the Illuminati followers, defeating most of them. But more still kept on coming and Sam and Sonja were starting to get overwhelmed.

Just then two golden daggers stabbed one of the followers of Azazel and he fell to the ground. Sam and Sonja both turned and it was revealed that Danny and Luke had arrived to the Eiffel Tower to help them. Danny and Luke did front flips to join Sam and Sonja. Then Danny said,

"We thought you guys could use a hand."

"Well, thanks for showing up fashionably late again, Danny." Sam replied.

"Hey, we couldn't just let you guys have all the fun now could we?" Danny shouted.

All four of them began to beat back the followers of Azazel until there were none left. Danny and Sam then turned to Luke and Sonja. Then Luke said,

"Sonja, do you have the first piece of the Spear?"

"Of course."

Then she pulled out a brown scroll and inside was a black staff with golden rings attached to it. As all four descendants held the piece, thunder and lightning echoed throughout the city of Paris. All four of them smiled. Then Luke said, "One piece down and two more to go."

As the Descendants walked away from the Eiffel Tower, Azazel was looking on from afar, frustrated that the Descendants defeated his followers again. "How could a group of teenagers be powerful enough to defeat my followers of master?" He thought. Then he realized that he underestimated The Descendants and their team work. If Azazel was going to defeat them, he was going to have to separated them from each other.

Chapter 12: Aftermath and Departure to China

After the epic and fantastic battle in Paris and getting the first piece of the Spear of Destiny, Luke, Sonja, and Sam all wanted to immediately find the second piece of the Spear. But Danny told them that they had to rest in order to save some energy as they just battled Azazel's followers.

"Look guys, I know you want to find the second piece of the Spear, but we have to rest. We just got through an epic battle with the Illuminati. We don't want to waste our energy immediately looking for the next piece and not having a plan." Danny said.

"Danny's right. As much as we were excited to fulfill our mission to stop the Illuminati, we have to be vigilant and come up with a strategy." Luke replied.

"Why can't we just go kill the demon Azazel wouldn't that make things easier. It would be like cutting the head of a snake" Sam said.

"Because we were barely able to defeat twenty Illuminati followers even with all four of us together. If we try to go after them now when we're weakened, we most likely will be killed." Luke said.

"Plus before the battle Azazel mentioned that his master demanded the piece of the spear. We need to find out who that is." Sonja said

Sam sighed then said, "Alright fine, I'll pitch in. How do we defeat Azazel together?"

Danny smiled and said, "Well, from what we've seen so far, Azazel only shows up when we find a piece of the Spear. So, we need to find the next piece and take him down."

"But Danny, we did that already and we nearly got defeated by them. As much as I hate to admit it, we were overwhelmed." Sam responded.

"You're right, but this time we will expect them to attack us when we find the piece and we'll be ready for them." Danny replied.

"We could set traps for them and take them on separately." Luke proposed.

"Yeah, but how are we going to do that? I mean, they are going to follow the command of Azazel." Sonja said.

"Leave that to me, let's just say I'm great with disguises." Luke said.

"Great, now let's rest in Paris for a few days and then we head out to China." Danny replied.

With their plan set in motion and their resolve in motion, the Descendants rest in Paris for a couple of days. Then Danny uses his teleportation to get them to China.

Chapter 13: Arrival in China!

Luke was awake while the others were asleep. For some reason, he couldn't sleep as well as the others. There was a sense of worry in Luke about this mission. "What if something goes wrong?" He thought. Ever since they arrived in China. Luke has been getting visions of the team battling Azazel and one of them getting stabbed in the chest. "What could this mean?" Luke thought. At first, he thought it was a dream, but he knew better. It was as if God was showing him what was going to happen. As Luke was in his thought process, and hand gripped his shoulder. Luke turned, and it was his cousin Danny who was awake.

"Can't sleep?" Danny said.

"No, Danny, I'm having visions and they are keeping me awake." Luke said.

"What kind of visions?" Danny replied.

"The kind that seem to be prophetic visions. In one of them we are battling the Illuminati in an epic battle and this time one of us gets stabbed." Luke said.

"Well Luke, God is showing you something important." Danny stated.

"Yeah, but the visions seem so real and I'm worried that—"

"Listen, Luke we'll be fine on this mission, relax. We have each other's back just in case something does happen."

Then Danny left Luke's presence and went to sleep. Luke thought about the words Danny spoke to him and was finally able to rest as well.

When Luke finally woke up and he was in a hotel with a picture of the Great Wall of China, as well as a painting of a winged figure pointing his finger at the wall. Luke then saw a figure looking at him. At first it was blurry, but after wiping his eyes he saw Danny.

"You talk when you sleep dude." Danny said.

Luke smiled, then said, "How long was I out?"

"We arrived in China on Wednesday and it is now Thursday. Dude, you're one heavy sleeper."

"Yeah, I know, so any luck finding the second piece of the Spear?" Luke asked.

"No, Sam and Sonja are out checking out China, well specifically, the Chinese library, to see if there are any plans of the Great Wall to see where the second piece of the Spear might be."

"That's good, how is that search going?"

"They haven't gotten back yet."

Just then Sam and Sonja appeared. Luke could tell that they both seemed to be out of breath. Sam went into the kitchen to the refrigerator and took a drink of water. After a few drinks to regain his breath, he spoke.

"Hey guys, we found some information on where the second piece might be. It's inside the Great wall of China."

"Inside it; are you kidding me?"

"No, I'm dead serious bro. Apparently, Matthew's comrades wanted to make sure the Spear would be impossible to unite. We have to dig into the foundation of the Wall to find the piece." Sam replied.

"Well, this is going to be a real pain, but we have to fulfill God's mission so when can we start."

"There's a field trip to The Great Wall in about twenty minutes."

"Great, let's go."

"Hold on, we can't go on a mission on an empty stomach."

Chapter 14: The Illuminati Make Their Move

As the Descendants walked out of the Hotel getting ready go on a field trip to the Great Wall of China, a man was watching them from afar. His attire was a red hood with battle armor on that resembled the ancient Chinese culture. He was going to have to blend in if he was going to watch over the four of them. He crouched under the piece of the window as he didn't want to draw the Descendants' attention. He had no complains about it as he knew his objective. He had to keep an eye on the Descendants per his employer's orders. Then he pressed tiny button on the binoculars to zoom in on the teenagers and one by one took pictures of the four of them. He watched as the four teenagers got onto the bus and rode away. As the bus started to move, the man took a picture of the license plate placed on the back of the bus. He made sure he had the license plate right; he said it three times in his head.

"Okay, I got it 529440 China." He thought. He remembered to take out his phone after tracking down the teenagers. He turned on his android phone and after a few seconds, he dialed a specific number by his employer; 853-980-4411. After a short ring, a heavy voice answered the phone.

"Are they on the move?"

"Yes, they're headed towards The Great Wall of China, just as you predicted."

"Good, you get your reward of one million dollars when you head back to your apartment Mr. Jones. You have done well."

"Thank you, Master Azazel and Hail the Evil One!"

"Hail him indeed." Azazel replied.

Mr. Jones then ended the call and began to head back to his apartment to collect his reward. He then gave what seemed to be a devilish grin across his face. He knew that very soon he would be the richest man alive.

Far from Mr. Jones' location, in a Chinese bank, Azazel closed the phone and turned around to ten assassins dressed in ninja attire with 666 branded on their arms kneeling before him. He then smiled as he knew Mr. Jones would prove to be useful and all it took was a simple suggestion of money and he completely ran with his plan. "Typical humans to obsessed with greed over objectionable things that there blinded by it." He thought. Azazel had a smile on his face as he knew Mr. Jones would be easily manipulated by money and now his usefulness was at an end. It was time to tie up loose ends. He had a camera installed in Mr. Jones' apartment, as well as a bomb to blow it up. He could see outside the apartment that he had just arrived and headed for the door. As soon as he unlocked the door and twisted the door knob, the bomb went off and Mr. Jones was officially dead.

"A pleasure doing business with you Mr. Jones." Azazel thought. He let out a small laugh. He had enjoyed seeing the demise of pathetic humans. "What does God see in these pathetic parasites?" He thought. He brushed the topic off and turned to his assassins.

"My children, it is time to fulfill your part in this mission to bring a One World Government. I have trained each and every one of you by hand. Your mission is to overwhelm and capture one of the Descendants and bring them to me, leave the others alive and they will be dealt with. Is that clear?"

At the same time, all ten of the assassins said, "Yes, Master Azazel."

"Good, now all of you go and do what needs to be done."

At once, all ten of the assassins jumped out of the bank and started to run free run across China to fulfill their mission. Azazel smiled and said,

"Those four teenagers won't know what's coming to them this time."

Chapter 15: Preparing for the Mission

Sam was listening to music while on the tour bus to the Great Wall of China. He knew the ride was going to be long, but he didn't expect it to be two hours long. He managed to listen to Drake's album, Views, four times while on the bus. He also could hear his stomach growling and he knew that if he didn't eat within a few more minutes, he would be starving. While trying to suppress his hunger, Sam took a glance at the country of China. He was amazed on how the buildings were different from the United States. Everything was bigger than in the United States. All of the buildings were as tall as a skyscraper and there was a parade in the street, with a dragon mascot as the center of attention. Everybody was gathered around it and people were singing and dancing. Sam began to show a quick smile on his face. "At least they having fun," he thought.

Just then, the bus arrived at the famous Great Wall of China. The bus driver began to speak in Chinese, but Sam could understand what he was saying. The language in his head was translated to Hebrew and then in English. He was telling the passengers to get off the bus and that they arrived.

At once, everybody got off the bus, along with Sam, Danny, Sonja, and Luke. After all four of them got off the bus, Luke took out the blueprints of the Great Wall and turned to everyone and said,

"Alright, everybody knows the mission. Fan out and search for the second piece."

"Alright, let's have some fun and beat up some more of Azazel's followers." Sonja said.

"I'm with you sister. Amen to that." Sam replied.

You guys, can we please take the mission seriously?" Danny responded.

"Relax Danny, we got this we'll find the second piece with ease." Sam replied.

"Like you did in Paris? Yeah, Sam that was a real breeze, huh?" Danny said.

"You two enough, let's just focus on the mission at hand and find the piece." Luke said.

"Fine!" Danny and Sam said at the same time.

Then all four Descendants went towards the Great Wall of China to search for the second piece of the Spear.

Chapter 16: The Second Piece Found

As Danny, Sam, Luke, and Sonja walked through the Great Wall of China, they all began to look around. For some reason, they were surprised. It could have been due to the fact that the wall was over a thousand years old and it felt like a giant maze, filled with secret passage entrances and hidden items. It's no coincidence that the Allied Forces used this place to keep the piece of the artifact well hidden. It was the perfect place to keep it safe. Normally, it would take a regular person decades to figure out the inner working of this place. But for the Descendants, this was like a scavenger hunt. After a few minutes of walking together, all four of them stopped at the same time. When they stopped, they could feel the wind passing through them. With sheer clarity in his voice, Luke shouted, "Now let the search begin!"

At once, all four of the Descendants took out their respected artifacts and weapons and they began to glow in a flash of pure light. As in Paris, discovered by Sonja and Sam, whenever the weapons of God gathered together to find another heavenly weapon, it was almost as if the artifacts become a GPS guide to it. The Spear of Destiny was no exception. All four of them began to run together in a straight path as they headed towards the second piece. At the same time, Sonja and Sam jumped on the two opposing sides of the wall on top of pillars. They began to run alongside Danny and Luke who were both running the same way.

As they kept on running and stepped ever so closer to the Spear, the artifacts on their bodies began to glow even brighter. The four of them kept on running, turning from corner to corner with ease until finally, their artifacts grew so bright that they started to become blinded by its spectacular presence. Each one of them knew that this was the spot of the second piece. But each of them looked around and no a piece of the Spear was in sight. Luke looked at his artifact as it was still glowing burning hot in the presence of such power. He knew that the piece was here. It was probably hidden beneath their feet. He turned to Sam and nodded his head. Immediately, bricks on the wall opened up and arrows started flying out of nowhere. Danny and Sonja used their weapons to block the arrows that were aimed at Sam. While Sam continued to use his superhuman strength to punch into the wall beneath them, a boulder appeared rolling down towards them. Then Luke stepped in and reached out both hands to stop the boulder. As Sam continued, his punches were so loud and powerful that they began to cause tremors in the wall all around them, as if a small earthquake had emerged.

Sam continued to punch into the wall, with each punch he made, he became increasingly more powerful. After a few minutes of punching into the wall, he stopped as a glowing object began to surface right before his eyes. He grabbed the glowing object with his bare hands. At once, he could feel the immense power with the second piece as it was increasing his strength and healing his injured knuckles from the punches he delivered earlier. Sam then turned to Sonja who took out the first piece that they got from Paris from her backpack. Sonja took the first piece inside the scroll and started to unwrap it.

As the unwrapping of the piece was complete, Sonja handed the piece over to Sam. Sam could see that both pieces were glowing in each other's presence. Then he put the two pieces together. Suddenly thunder and lightning could be seen over the Great Wall of China, as thunder clouds appeared in response to the pieces of the Spear being united. Then Sam watched as a partial inscription began to appear in Hebrew, but Sam couldn't read it for some reason. It was probably due to the Spear being incomplete. Then the thunder and lightning stopped. After a few minutes of silence, Sam said, "Well, that was more than I expected." All four of them began to laugh when suddenly a mysterious voice said, "You're going to have a few more surprises descendant of Samson."

Immediately, all four of them turned around and one by one ten people in red hooded figures and battle armor appeared surrounding them in a circle. Each one of the figures had a variety of weapons that included swords, daggers, and a symbol on their arm of the mark 666.

Sam displayed a slight smile on his face, then in a nostalgic voice said, "Well, this is the type of unexpected I'm going to enjoy."

Chapter 17: A Comrade Captured

Sam was gripping his weapon tightly as he was being surrounded by ten assassins working for Azazel. Sam smiled, he loved this feeling of nostalgia. The sights, the sounds of constant punching and kicking made him excited like never before. This is what he loves and is passionate about; the thrill of battle. Sam watched as Danny, Sonja, and Luke took out their artifacts and turned them into weapons, just like at the football field. There was a chilling feeling in the air as all four of the Descendants were being surrounded. Luke finally summoned the courage to speak and said,

"Guys, we'll take them on together as a team. Sam you go in slowly and I'll—"

"No, screw this, I'm taking them now!" Sam interrupted.

Sam, wasting no time at all, began to rush towards the assassins, with all his might, he blocked out all other sounds, other than his own breathing. In the background, he could barely hear what Luke said, "Sam, wait what are you doing?" Sam was doing what he did best—fighting. As he got closer to the assassins he launched into the air and threw his dagger at one of the assassins, but he dodged the attack with just a slight tilt of the head. While the assassins were distracted, Sonja, Luke, and Danny charged at the assassins with powerful kicks that sent them back a few feet. Sam then returned to the ground.

Danny, Sonja, and Luke all rushed to Sam's side. The assassins then formed together side by side as well.

Then Luke said, "Sam, are you ready to work with the team now?"

"Hey, that was the plan all along right?" Sam replied.

Luke smiled, "It seems you have brains as well as bronze."

Then all four of the Descendants charged at the ten assassins. The assassins charged at them as well. Each Descendant was gripping their weapon tightly as they were running towards the enemy. All of the weapons of each group clashed against each other at the same time. Sam pretended to swing his sword to attack to the leg, but it was really a distraction as the assassin blocked the attack with relative ease. Sam then punched the assassin in the face with his strength and sent him flying back into the wall. Sam watched as Danny battled three assassins at once. He was being calm and cautious as he effortlessly blocked all of their blows. He managed to jump up in the air and perform as spin kick towards their heads, knocking them out. Sonja was using the Staff of Moses to perform a powerful blast of light to the assassins, taking them down as well. It seemed like the Descendants were going to win.

But after five more minutes of fighting, the Descendants were being overwhelmed by the sheer skill of the assassins. Then Luke said,

"We should retreat."

"No, we can take these fools." Sam replied.

As Sam finished his sentence, one of the assassins reached out his hand. Sonja suddenly couldn't move. She was frozen in place and then lifted up in the air, she floated towards the assassin's hand. She was being gripped by the throat and she was clearly choking. The assassin said, "Drop your weapons or she dies."

The Descendants did so, but Sonja was still in the air being strangled. The assassin then smiled and said, "If you want to see your friend again bring us the second piece of the Spear and she will live." Then in a fiery blaze appeared and the ten assassins and Sonja were gone. At once Sam, Danny, and Luke all stared at each other. The look on each of their faces was clear as day. "What happened?"

Chapter 18: The Rescue

Luke, Danny, and Sam stood there bewildered, as they were still processing what just happened. Sonja was captured by the Illuminati and she is in danger. Danny and Luke knew this would happen and they should have done more. Danny and Luke watched as Sam stood silently for five minutes. He suddenly realized that he can't always work alone and that sometimes you need to work with other people as a team. Then, he turned to Danny and Luke with a menacing glare on his eyes. For the first time, Danny was afraid of seeing Sam. He had never been like this before, normally he would have an optimistic "let's go after the enemy" type of attitude, but the facial expression right now was that of pure rage and seriousness. Sam walked over towards Luke and Danny and said,

"You know we have to work together and get her back right?"

"Of course, which is why I took precautions." Luke replied.

Then Luke got out his android phone and looked at the GPS signal. It seemed to be coming from the Chinese bank, CITIC. Their location was five miles from the Great Wall. Luke was pleased. Then he showed his phone to Sam. After seeing the phone, Sam was in sheer shock.

"How? When did you—"

"I took the liberty of placing a homing beacon on one of the assassins during our epic confrontation with them. That way if one of us got captured, we could track the location and be rescued." Luke replied.

"Luke, dude, you are the one of the smartest people I know." Danny said.

"Well, I am a descendant of Solomon after all."

"Great, now that we have their location, let's go rescue Sonja. Luke, what's the plan?" Sam said.

Danny and Luke glanced at each other for a moment. "Looks like Sam has learned to work with others." Danny thought. Then Luke said, "Well, I'm glad you asked Sam. Okay guys, here's what we're going to do."

At the Chinese bank, CITIC, Sonja was being carried by two guys towards a mysterious figure. Sonja quickly recognized who it was; the demon, Azazel, smiling with a devilish glare across his face. Sonja was placed in a chair with her hands tied behind her back. Azazel walked over to the three of them and said,

"You may leave us." Azazel said to the assassins, in a cold calculating voice.

"Yes master," said the two assassins at the same time.

Then they left Azazel and Sonja in the main banking floor. Azazel then approached Sonja and said,

"You know, it's useless to fight against my master. When his followers in the Illuminati rule the world, there will be a New World Order."

"Yeah, an Order of complete chaos" Sonja replied.

"His New World Order will have you fifthly humans wiped out from existence, that sound good to me." Azazel said.

"You mentioned in our last battle that you had a master. Who is he?" Sonja asked.

Azazel smirked and said, "He has so many names it's hard to keep track of all of them. But don't worry child you will find out soon enough. You know I wasn't always a demon I was once an angel of the Lord. I remember how the universe was created and how we all sang for joy. It was magnificent"

Azazel then turned towards the window and looked outward. Then he continued, "This was truly the last perfect handwork of God." Azazel said in amazement. As Azazel was standing there, Sonja pulled out one of her knives and started to untie herself. Azazel then turned back to Sonja and said,

"Then God had to create you, the little humans, and he had the audacity to ask all of us to bow down before you. Huh, to love you more than him. At that moment, I stopped serving God and I began to serve my master The

Evil One. I remember how beautiful he was as he defied our father's order. There was such charisma and passion within his voice; I wanted to follow him. Plus, he was right. God gave you our birthright. We were here first, we were his children first, and you humans should love us not the other way around. After my master's fall, along with me and my other comrades who supported him in his rebellion were casted into hell, He thanked me for my service. He made me into something better; a demon, where I don't have to follow the demands of a divine fool. Who loves something so weak and flawed? It's ridiculous."

"So this is all about you and your master, as well as other demons reclaiming your birthright, is that it? " Sonja replied.

"Yes, and soon we will have our victory!" Azazel exclaimed.

"You know my friends and I won't let that happen. They'll be coming for me."

Azazel grinned as he got in Sonja's face and said, "Oh, I'm counting on it."

Suddenly, Sonja broke free and stabbed Azazel in the eye then used all her strength to kick him in the face sending him across the room. Sonja ran towards the door, but Azazel reached out his hand and stopped her movement.

He moved his hand towards the right side of the room sending Sonja flying across the room and hitting against the wall. He walked over towards her, smiled and said,

"Nice try girl, but did you really think it was going to be that easy?"

"No, but it's going to get a lot harder in a minute."

Then an alarm goes off and Azazel looks at the cameras. He could see a boy lifting up one of his soldiers and throwing him across the room. Then the boy looked towards the camera and said, "Hey, Azazel, if you want to fight me, I'm right here." Azazel smiled and headed down to the entrance.

Sam was breathing hard and waiting patiently for Azazel to come down. If Azazel has any type of ego he will come to face him. "He probably won't even view me as a threat." He thought. As he could hear the elevator coming down, he took out the Jawbone of Samson and gripped it tightly in his hand—he was ready for battle.

As the elevator shaft opened, Sam wasting no time at all, rushed towards it, but a powerful shock wave sent him flying across the wall. He looked up to see what caused such force only for the source of it to be Azazel's hand.

Sam was held against the wall by Azazel's hand alone. But Sam could feel the Jawbone of Samson flowing through him, as it is increasing his strength. He was able to move his body a little bit more each time he took a step. Azazel tried to use his telekinesis to put Sam on the wall again, but Sam kept on moving towards him. Azazel then stopped, as he realized it was useless. Sam swung the Jawbone at Azazel's face twice, but the demon was able to dodge both attacks with relative ease. Azazel kicked Sam in the stomach, sending him against the wall, leaving a huge crack in it. Then the demon then walked over to Sam and picked him up by the throat, but Sam punched him in the face, sending him back a few feet. Sam rushed to Azazel to deliver a kick. Before the blow could even be delivered, the demon caught Sam's leg and threw him into another wall, this time making a huge hole into it. Azazel walked over to Sam and took out his sword. He grabbed Sam and was about to deliver the final blow. Suddenly a voice said, "Hey Azazel!" Azazel turned and he was met by a powerful blast of light that blasted him into the bank's ATM. Then Sam turned left to see that it was Sonja who used her Staff of Moses. Danny and Luke were with her side by side.

Sam smiled and said, "You guys took way to long in that rescue."

"Well, we had some hold up of ten assassins to deal with, so don't rush us too much." Luke said.

Danny walked over to Sam to help him up. Sonja and Luke both walked towards them. Luke then said, "Alright, now that our friend, Sonja, has successfully been rescued, let's find the last piece of the Spear of Destiny." Then all four Descendants walked out of the building together to find the last piece of the Spear where ironically, it was first discovered; Jerusalem.

Chapter 19: The Last Piece

After the confrontation in the Chinese Bank with Azazel, Luke figured the rest of the team needed rest before they boarded the plane to Israel. This will be the final part of the mission, finding the last piece of the Spear of Destiny. "All the obstacles that we've had to overcome and now it's come to this." Luke thought. Ever since he has worked with all three of his comrades, sitting laying on the beds resting, he knew all four of them were met to be a team. Also, in his time of connecting with them, he grew to respect them and gain their friendship along the way. Soon, their mission will be completed and Luke would not have it any other way. Luke stared at the team one last time before he laid down and went to sleep.

❖--

The sun came shining brightly into the hotel. As Danny woke up, he looked to see that the rest of the team had just woke up as well. Danny put on his favorite clothes; blue jeans, black Nike shoes, and a blue shirt that said "Just be yourself." Then he got his bags and waited on the couch. After a few minutes, one by one, the Descendants were ready to leave China. Realizing that they need to head to Israel immediately, Danny, Sam, and Sonja started to walk out of the hotel room. Then the four of them gather together and Danny teleported them to Jerusalem.

As they all arrived in Israel thanks to Danny's powers Sonja needed rest from walking so she asked Danny to get a cab, so they can drive towards the city of Jerusalem. Sam was right next to her and he was listening to music. Danny and Luke were right behind them seated next to each other as well. At once, they all looked towards each other and smiled as a heavy feeling grew inside of them all. This is where it all happened, where their ancestors did their mighty deeds in the name of God; in the Middle

East. But the time for nostalgia was over. They were here for one thing and they knew what they had to do.

On the way to a hotel in Jerusalem, they saw board posters of President Netanyahu talking about going to war with Palestine. They were also a news interview of him claiming that it is a part of God's plan to have Israel kill off the Palestine people. In it, he said, "It's biblical. For thousands of years, we Israelites have fought the Palestinians since the time of Isaac and Ishamel. Now the war needs to end."

Danny and Sam both were annoyed with the response of Israel's President and turned off the TV. Sonja didn't blame them, another politician calling for a holy war, what else is new? "At least he's not Donald Trump," she thought.

Just then, they had arrived at the hotel. One by one, Luke, Sonja, Danny, and Sam all got out of the car and walked into the hotel. As they walked in, Luke saw a list of all current events in Israel on a paper. It said that there was a tour guide of the temple of Jerusalem from 5 p.m. to 8 p.m. Danny got their room key; room 208. The four of them headed towards the elevator and went to the room. When they got inside Luke said,

"Okay, the tour guide to the temple of Jerusalem is from 5 p.m. until 8 p.m. I figure if we go to the temple at 9 p.m., we will have a chance to get the final piece of the Spear."

"Sounds like a plan oh fearless leader." Sam said.

"Actually, it was Danny's idea, but thanks anyway." Luke said.

"Really Danny, you should lead us more often." Sam replied.

"Maybe I will." Danny said with a smile across his face.

With that, the Descendants waited patiently as the sunset was turning into night. In a few hours, they would be heading towards the holy temple of Jerusalem or what's left of it.

❖---

As 9 p.m. approached, Danny, along with Luke, Sam, and Sonja where all dressed in black body armor with three golden weapons. They were outside the remains of the temple of Jerusalem. As they walked into the ruins of the temple, their artifacts glowed brightly and as they got closer to the location of the final piece, it beamed with light. After looking for a few minutes, the four of them watched as their artifacts glowed so bright that they couldn't even bear it. Danny looked towards Sam who then removed a huge boulder and found a golden crusted box. Luke opened it and a beam of golden light was radiating from it. Luke grabbed the last piece of the Spear. It was a black lance with a golden frame around it. Then he turned to Danny. Danny took his backpack and grabbed the other two pieces of the Spear. Luke gave the final piece to Danny and he put them together. Immediately following, was a sudden thunder cloud, followed by countless lighting strikes around the temple. The cloud stretched out as if it was over the entire would for a moment and emulating the divine power of the Spear. The team looked around to see the divine power of the Spear of Destiny. On the newly completed Spear, the inscription that Sam saw earlier came again. This time he, along with the others could read it. It read, "THE SPEAR OF THE MESSIAH."

Luke, Sam, Danny, and Sonja all could feel the divine power of the Spear of Destiny, simply by being in the artifact's presence. It was nothing compared to how

Danny felt—he was shaking in excitement as he held the spear. The he said,

"I've never felt this much power before."

"Me neither Danny." Sam said.

Then a familiar voice said, "Well done Descendants you did all my work for me."

All four of them turned around to see Azazel in silver battle armor, as well as forty demons with black eyes and horns on their heads, and twelve hellhounds. All four Descendants took out their weapons, except for Danny, he had the Spear of Destiny in his hands. With exhilaration he said, "Team, let this be our final battle." With that, all four Descendants charged at Azazel's army.

Chapter 20: The Final Battle!

Danny was running at Azazel's army as fast as he possibly could. He could still feel the power of the Spear as well as the power of the Holy Spirit flowing through him and slowly but surely, he pointed the legendary Spear down with the sharp tip of it in the front of him. His closest friends who had been gifted with special abilities were right beside him. Azazel looked to his army and said, "Attack! Crush them and kill them all."

With that, his army charged at Danny and his friends. One by one, they took out their weapons running towards them. Both sides were screaming with all their might. There was a sense of exhilaration in the air. Danny knew this was it his first moment of leading his friends into battle. One by one, the Descendants took off their black hoods and revealed golden battle armor that matched their weapons. As both armies went closer and closer towards each other, there was a chill silence in the air. With a few more steps, both armies clashed with each other.

There were sounds of swords clashing against each other. Sam was lifting, using his superhuman strength to throw the soldiers into the walls of the temple. He delivered a punch to another one sending him flying back against his other comrades, which sent them all crashing and falling to the ground. Sonja used the Staff of Moses to create a powerful blast of light. Luke was surrounded by enemies and he had two daggers. One enemy tried to attack him from behind, but Luke dodged and took the arm of the attacker and flipped him over towards the other. He stretched out his arms and sent a powerful shockwave towards the others, sending them into the ruins of the temple. Then Luke smiled, he had just discovered a new ability; telekinesis.

Danny used the Spear to stab the soldiers in front of him. One of them tried to swing a sword at his head, but he dodged it and stabbed him right in the chest, turning the demon to ash. Danny stabbed two other demons and then he took the Spear and spun it in the air, and swung it to the right, creating a powerful blast of electricity to the other demons. He pointed the Spear forward and ran with it, stabbing countless others. Then Danny saw Azazel at the top of the temple. Just as Sam defeated the last hellhound that jumped on him, he saw Danny and Azazel staring at each other and leaped towards them—landing alongside Danny.

"Hey Danny, what do say we teach this demon of hell a lesson?" Sam said.

"No problem Sam." Danny replied.

Azazel smiled and said, "I'm going to enjoy this."

At the same time, Danny and Sam charged at Azazel. They both went for a punch to his chest, but he blocked their blows with both of his hands. Then Danny and Sam kicked him in the chest sending him flying backwards in a roll. Danny and Sam both ran to Azazel and attacked him one on one. Danny went for a kick, but Azazel grabbed his leg and threw him to the wall. He was about to attack Danny, but he was punched by Sam. Then Sonja and Luke joined the fight as well by delivering a kick to Azazel sending him into a pillar.

"We thought you two could use a hand." Sonja said.

"Well thanks." Sam replied.

Danny and Luke joined Sonja and Sam. Azazel got out of the wreckage, turned to his enemies and charged at them. Luke and Sonja tried to stab him with their weapons, but he blocked them and double kicked them in the stomach sending them back. He then grabbed Danny by the throat and punched him in the face before he could react. He telekinetically grabbed Sam in the air holding him. Azazel then took out his sword and pulled Sam towards him and stabbed in him the stomach. Danny, Sonja, and Luke all watched in horror as Sam fell to the ground not moving. Immediately all three of them rush towards him. Using their heighten senses they could tell that he was barely alive. Then Azazel told his remaining army to charge at the team. Suddenly, Danny saw what appeared to be a beam of light falling from the sky and landing right in front of the Descendants. As it landed, on impact, the demons went flying back and the bright white light disappeared revealing a man. He had a white robe with silver battle armor and a glowing white sword. He charged at the rest of the demons and killed them off one by one with incredible ease. He also had the ability of kill demons with the snap of his fingers or with a touch on their forehead. The man continued to kill off the demons until the rest of them were turned to ash. He then turned towards Azazel, reached out his hand, and blasted him in a beam of light.

Then the mysterious man walked towards the four Descendants and kneeled before a badly wounded Sam. Danny tried to stop him, but the man said, "It's okay Danny Wallace. I can help heal your friend."

Danny paused and let the man touch Sam. In a flash of light, the fatal blow to him was healed. Danny helped Sam up. All four Descendants turned toward the figure. Danny spoke first and said,

"Who are you and more importantly what are you?"

The man smiled and said, "My name is Zadkiel and to put it simply, I'm and angel of the Lord." The Descendants watched as Zadkiel's wings came out. There was a glowing of pure white light around them that temperamentally blinded them, followed by a brief sound of thunder and lighting. At the same time Danny, Sam, Sonja, and Luke all backed away from the angel. Zadkiel then smiled and said,

"Do not be afraid, for I am a warrior for God like all four of you are."

Danny said, "Zadkiel, I can't thank you enough for helping us. We were in a pretty messed up situation there, but I have to ask you this: Why did you do it, why did you save us?"

"Because my Father, God, commanded it; he has work for you. By stopping Azazel here, we just prevented him from breaking one of the seven seals."

"The seven seals to what?" Danny replied.

"To free the Evil One. You have heard that Azazel had a master well his master is none other than Lucifer. You should think of the seals as locks on a door and when all of them break, Lucifer will be free from Hell and the apocalypse begins."

The

End

Epilogue

Danny, along with Sam, Luke, and Sonja, were walking down a dark secret tunnel. They had never seen or known about this part of Jerusalem and they all seemed nervous about where they were going. They had tried asking Zadkiel a bunch of times where they were being led to, but he would not answer; he said it was a surprise. After a few minutes of walking, there was a sudden halt. Zadkiel appeared to have stopped in front of them. He went up to a brick wall. Then he turned to Danny and said, "Danny Wallace, come place your hand on this wall."

Without question, Danny walked over to the dead end brick wall in front of him and placed his left hand on the wall. Suddenly, the brick pushed in and the wall opened upwards. Immediately, Danny, along with Sam, Sonja, and Luke, saw huge amounts of space within the wall. The all stepped in and looked around. They could see that there was a bunch of swords and crossbows and other types of weaponry. There was also a bunch of new furniture and a crest that had a red cross on it in the middle of the floor, along with the battle armor. They all seemed to recognize it as the Knights Templar's hideout.

"This is where we will be training for the battle that is to come with the Dark Ones. We will harness your powers and unlock new ones with the spark of his power inside you. Father gave me specific instructions to help you develop your powers and help you find the artifact that is next on the Illuminati's list. " Zadkiel said.

"What's the next item?" Sonja asked.

"Sonja, I'm glad you asked because you have a deep connection to it. The item is called the Ark of the Covenant."

Acknowledgments

I would like to thank all my friends and family who supported me in making this book. I would also like to thank my friends who encouraged me to get this book published. My hope is that everybody who supported me can witness the potential and greatness of this book series.

Thank you.

Sequel

Witness the journey of the Descendants continue as they go up against an enemy that has the power to bring the world to its knees. Will the Descendants stop the Dark Ones before it is too late? Find out in the book titled,

"The Descendants Book 2: The Ark of the Covenant."

About The Author

Hello there! My name is Philip Daniel Bell and I am a published author. I am creating a book series called The Descendants. It is about four teenagers that are called by God and are tasked with stopping The Illuminati from releasing Lucifer from Hell and creating The New World Order! The total in this book series is five books. Each book with be jam packed with Action and Adventure and will answer more questions in this series. The first book is called The Descendants: The Spear of Destiny and the second book is called The Descendants: The Ark of The Covenant.

If you want to contact me my phone number is 206-775-0551

Email : danielbell3498@gmail.com

Instagram: dabbindanny1

Made in the USA
Columbia, SC
22 February 2019